a picture book by William Stobbs

The Crock of Gold

BEING "THE PEDLAR OF SWAFFHAM" BY JOSEPH JACOBS

FOLLETT PUBLISHING COMPANY • CHICAGO

ISBN 0-695-80213-5 Trade binding
ISBN 0-695-40213-7 Titan binding

Library of Congress Catalog Card Number: 70-149499

7931

First Printing

In the old days, when London Bridge was lined with shops from one end to the other, and salmon swam under the arches,

there lived at Swaffham,
in Norfolk, a poor pedlar.

He'd much ado to make his living, trudging
about with his pack at his back and his dog at
his heels, and at the close of the day's labour
was but too glad to sit down and sleep.

Now it fell out that one night he dreamed
a dream, and therein he saw the great bridge
of London town, and it sounded in his ears
that if he went there he should hear joyful news.

He made little count of the dream, but on
the following night it came back to him,
and again on the third night.

Then he said within himself, "I must needs try the issue of it," and so he trudged up to London town.

Long was the way and right glad was he
when he stood on the great bridge and
saw the tall houses on right hand and left,
and had glimpses of the water running
and the ships sailing by.

All day long he paced to and fro, but he heard
nothing that might yield him comfort.

And again on the morrow he stood and he
gazed—he paced afresh the length of
London Bridge, but naught did he see
and naught did he hear.

Now the third day being come, as he still stood and gazed, a shopkeeper hard by spoke to him.

"Friend," said he, "I wonder much at your fruitless standing. Have you no wares to sell?"

"No, indeed," quoth the pedlar.

"And you do not beg for alms?"

"Not so long as I can keep myself."

"Then what, I pray thee, dost thou want here, and what may thy business be?"

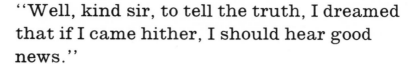

"Well, kind sir, to tell the truth, I dreamed that if I came hither, I should hear good news."

Right heartily did the shopkeeper laugh.

"Nay, thou must be a fool to take a journey on such a silly errand. I'll tell thee, poor silly country fellow, that I myself dream too o'nights, and that last night I dreamt myself to be in Swaffham, a place clean unknown to me, but in Norfolk if I mistake not, and methought I was in an orchard behind a pedlar's house, and in that orchard was a great oak tree.

"Then meseemed that if I digged I should find beneath that tree a great treasure. But think you I'm such a fool as to take on me a long and wearisome journey and all for a silly dream? No, my good fellow, learn wit from a wiser man than thyself. Get thee home, and mind thy business."

When the pedlar heard this he spoke no word,
but was exceeding glad in himself, and returning
home speedily, digged underneath the great
oak tree, and found a prodigious great
treasure.

He grew exceeding rich, but he did not forget his duty in the pride of his riches. For he built up again the church at Swaffham, and when he died they put a statue of him therein all in stone with his pack at his back and his dog at his heels. And there it stands to this day to witness if I lie.